Kelly

W9-BJK-578

The Young Collector's
Illustrated Classics

Oliver Twist

By
Charles Dickens

Adapted by
Kathleen Costick

Contents

Chapter

1

The Workhouse

Every city in England, large or small, has a workhouse. It is there that poor people are taken from the streets to be fed, clothed, and given tiresome work to do. They are not fed very well—only enough to keep them from dying of hunger. One stormy night, in a city it is best not to name here, a boy was born in one of these very workhouses. He was to be called Oliver Twist.

Oliver was so frail when he was born that the workhouse doctor and the shriveled old woman who attended him were surprised that he lived. His first cries were thin and faint. When his pale, young

mother heard them, she raised herself feebly from her bed and said in a voice that could barely be heard, "Let me hold my child before I die."

The doctor quickly put the baby in her arms. She kissed his little forehead lovingly. Then she gazed around, shuddered, fell back—and died.

"It's all over now, Sally," the doctor said as he prepared to leave.

"Ah, poor dear, so it is!" said the old woman sadly.

"Such a pretty girl too, so delicate-looking," said the doctor. "She is not at all like the other women I see here. Where did she come from?"

"She was found lying in the street last night," replied the old woman. "She must have walked a long way because her shoes were worn to pieces. But who she is or where she came from, nobody knows."

The doctor shook his head sadly and said, "I wonder where the father of her child is. Perhaps he is dead, too. Ah well," he sighed as he put on his hat. "I must go. Goodnight, Sally."

"Goodnight, sir," the old woman muttered as she bent over the body of the young mother. The new baby now screamed so loudly that his little voice filled the room.

Oliver Twist grew into a pale, thin boy. He had a sad, wistful look about him. After he was born, he was sent to a

farmhouse which was really a workhouse for homeless, young children. It was run by a mean, stingy woman named Mrs. Mann. The children in her charge were always dirty and hungry. Every once in a while, one of the babies would fall from their cribs and tumble to the floor.

One day Oliver complained that he was hungry. As a punishment for this, Mrs. Mann locked him in the coal cellar. While Oliver sat in the dark on the cold stone steps, Mrs. Mann was startled to see someone she knew trying to open her garden gate.

"Oh no," she said to herself. "It's Bumble from the workhouse." She pulled Oliver out of the cellar and sent him upstairs. Then she ran out shouting, "Is that you, Mr. Bumble, sir? How glad I am to see you! The gate is locked so that none of my dear little children can wander away from me. I will open it for you in just one second."

"Do you think it proper, Mrs. Mann, to keep an officer from the workhouse waiting at your garden gate?" puffed Mr. Bumble. He was a fat man, and his face was pink and shiny after his long walk.

"Oh dear, Mr. Bumble, sir. I'm sure I

came just as soon as I could," Mrs. Mann replied meekly.

"All right then. Let's go in," said Mr. Bumble.

Mrs. Mann led him into a small parlor. Then she picked up a bottle and said with a glint in her eye, "You've had a long walk, Mr. Bumble. Would you care for a little drop of something to drink?"

Mr. Bumble looked at the bottle and said, "Well, really I shouldn't . . ."

"Just a drop, Mr. Bumble," said Mrs. Mann as she began to pour.

After Mr. Bumble had drained his glass, he took out a small notebook and said with great importance, "Oliver Twist is now nine years old. Although we offered a reward for information about him, we have never discovered whom his parents were."

"Why, who gave him his name then?" asked Mrs. Mann.

Mr. Bumble drew himself up proudly and said, "I did! We name our foundlings

in alphabetical order. The one before this was S, and I named him Stubble. This was T, and I named him Twist."

Mrs. Mann declared that he was very clever.

"Oliver is too old to stay here now," continued Mr. Bumble. "I have come to bring him back to the workhouse. Please fetch him at once."

A few minutes later, Oliver was being led away by Mr. Bumble, from the only home he had ever known.

Oliver felt terribly sad to leave the farmhouse. He had been unhappy there, but the other children were his friends. He felt very, very alone as he struggled to keep up with Mr. Bumble's huge steps.

Once inside the workhouse, Mr. Bumble handed Oliver to an old woman and left. He returned fifteen minutes later to say that it was "board" night, and that the "board" wanted to see Oliver.

Now Oliver had no idea that the workhouse was run by a group of men

called the "board of directors." So he was very surprised to hear that a board wanted to see him. When Mr. Bumble brought him into a room where nine fat men were sitting around a table, and told him to "bow to the board," he looked hastily around. Seeing no board except the table, Oliver decided to bow to that.

"What's your name, boy?" asked one gentleman. All the men looked sternly at Oliver, which frightened him so much he could hardly speak. Then Mr. Bumble rapped him on the head with his stick. Oliver had to fight to hold back his tears.

"Oliver Twist, sir," he answered in a low voice. A man in a white vest said Oliver was a fool.

Another man at the table asked, "You know you're an orphan, don't you? I mean, you know you've no father or mother to take care of you?"

"Yes sir," replied Oliver. Tears sprang to his eyes, but he could do nothing to stop them.

The first gentleman said, "You must live and work here. You will begin working tomorrow morning at six o'clock."

Oliver bowed again and was led to a room full of hard, narrow beds. He sobbed himself to sleep.

The people in the workhouse were not happy. They were hungry and miserable. They wanted to leave, but they had no money and no place to go. Because

they couldn't find work, they had to stay.

However, the "board of directors," who ran the workhouse, thought the poor people there were happy. The board wanted to make it more unpleasant in order to encourage some of them to leave. Soon after Oliver left the board room, they decided that the people should have only half as much food to eat.

For the next six months, Oliver worked at taking apart old ropes. The stringy fibers were separated and later used to stuff the cracks in ships to make them water-tight. He and the other boys were fed three bowls of thin gruel a day. They became almost wild with hunger. One boy was afraid that, unless he had more food to eat, he would wake up one night and find that he had eaten the boy in the bed next to him. He was big, and all the boys believed him. Something had to be done!

The boys met and decided that one of them should walk up to the master after supper and ask for more food. But who? They were all afraid. So, a small bundle of straws was made, one of which was much shorter than the rest. Each boy would take a straw out of the bundle. Whoever drew the short straw would have to ask the master for more.

One by one, the boys took their turns. Then it was Oliver's turn. His hand wavered for a moment over the straws— should he choose this one or that? Finally, he took one. It was the short straw!

Supper time came, and the boys were led into the big stone hall where they ate. The master stood at the front beside an enormous, iron pot of bubbling gruel. The boys waited in line for him to fill their bowls.

At the end of the meal, the boys whispered to each other and winked at Oliver. They nudged him with their feet. Oliver got up from the table and, with his bowl and spoon in his hands, walked towards the master. He was so hungry that he almost didn't care what happened to him. He felt reckless and very daring. Even so, he was a little surprised to hear himself say, in a voice that did not tremble, "Please, sir, I want some more."

The master turned very pale. He gazed at Oliver in astonishment. The boys were frozen with fear.

"What?" the master asked, blinking in disbelief.

"Please, sir," repeated Oliver, "I want some more."

Suddenly, the master hit him on the head with his ladle, and grabbed him so that he couldn't escape—all the time screaming loudly for help. Mr. Bumble came running in, waving his cane in front of him.

The directors were having another

meeting when Mr. Bumble burst into their room and exclaimed, "I beg your pardon, sirs, but Oliver Twist has just asked for more!"

The directors of the workhouse were horrified.

"For more?" asked a gentleman at the head of the table. "Excuse me, Mr. Bumble, but do you mean to say that, after he had eaten his bowl of gruel, he asked for more?"

"He did, sir," replied Mr. Bumble.

"I said that boy was a fool," a man in a white vest remarked proudly. "Now I say that he will most certainly hang someday!" Several of the other men nodded in agreement. They ordered Oliver to be locked in a room by himself.

The next morning, a sign was posted on the gate outside the workhouse. It offered a reward of five pounds to anyone

A
REWARD
of
£5

for anyone who will take a nine year old boy named Oliver Twist off the hands of the parish

who would take a nine-year-old boy named Oliver Twist. In other words, any person who needed a boy to work for him could have Oliver—and five pounds.

Oliver found himself a prisoner in a dark room. At night, when it was so dark that he could not even see his own hand in front of his face, he would press against the stone wall. In a strange way, the hard stone comforted him. It seemed to protect him from the black nothingness all around him and made him feel less lonely.

Every morning, he was shoved under a pump, and icy cold water was run over him. At supper time, he was placed on a platform in the dining hall and beaten with a cane by Mr. Bumble. All the boys were warned that if they didn't behave, they would be punished like Oliver Twist.

Chapter

2

In
the Shop

While the sign about Oliver was on the gate, a man covered with black soot wandered past the workhouse. He pulled a donkey along beside him. The man was a chimney sweep, and he seemed troubled about something. In fact, he owed a good deal of money to his landlord and could not think of a way to pay it.

The donkey stumbled in front of the workhouse, and the man turned and kicked it again and again, muttering curses at it. Suddenly, his eye caught sight of the sign on the gate. He stopped to read it. He grinned and scratched his stubby face.

"Five pounds!" he whispered to himself.

Just then, Mr. Bumble came and asked if he needed a boy to work for him. The man nodded.

"Then follow me," said Mr. Bumble.

Mr. Bumble took him to see the directors of the workhouse.

"It is very dangerous to clean chimneys," said one of the directors, when he heard that the man wanted to take Oliver Twist. "Many boys have become caught in

them and have smothered to death by smoke."

"Never mind," said the man in the white vest, "it's a good trade for a boy like Oliver Twist." The other men at the table laughed. They told Mr. Bumble to bring Oliver before a judge so that he could be signed over to the chimney sweep.

Later, in court, Oliver stood before a kindly judge who wore little round glasses on the end of his nose.

The judge asked the chimney sweep, "Will you take good care of this boy, sir, and teach him a trade?"

The chimney sweep grinned and nodded.

Oliver stared in horror at the man's cruel, ugly face. He was terrified to think he would have to work for him!

The judge had a pen ready to sign Oliver's papers, but he couldn't seem to find the ink. As he was looking for it, he chanced to raise his head and saw Oliver in front of him, wide-eyed with fear.

"My boy!" exclaimed the judge, leaning over his desk. "You look alarmed. What is the matter?"

Oliver clasped his hands together and begged the judge to do anything rather than send him away with that dreadful man. He said he would rather go back to the dark room and be beaten than go with him!

The judge turned to Mr. Bumble and said, "I refuse to sign this boy over to that man. Take him back to the workhouse . . . and treat him more kindly!"

Mr. Bumble tried to find someone else to take young Oliver—with no luck. One day, he happened to meet Mr. Sowerberry, the undertaker, who said,

"Hello, Mr. Bumble. I have just measured the woman who died last night at the workhouse. I will finish making her coffin as soon as I can."

Much to his surprise, Mr. Bumble soon learned that Mr. Sowerberry wanted Oliver Twist to work in his house and shop. It was all settled in a few hours. Oliver was brought to the coffin-maker's door that very evening.

Mr. Sowerberry's nasty wife took Oliver into the kitchen and gave him some scraps to eat. She showed him a place under the counter in the shop where he was to sleep, then she left him.

Oliver looked around fearfully. A half-finished coffin lay on a table in the middle of the shop. It was so gloomy in the room that Oliver almost expected to see some frightful creature get out of it and walk towards him. Against the wall was a long row of boards, all cut into the same coffin shape. They looked like a row of square-shouldered ghosts to Oliver.

Oliver was awakened in the morning by the sound of someone kicking at the front door of the shop.

"Open the door, will 'ya?" cried a voice outside.

Oliver opened the door and found himself face-to-face with a big boy who seemed to have very small eyes for such a large head.

"You don't know who I am, do you?"

the big boy growled at him.

"No sir, I don't," replied Oliver.

"I'm Noah Claypole, you little work-house brat, and I work here! You have to follow my orders. Now get that broom over there, and be quick about it!"

Noah Claypole shouted at Oliver and kicked him when they were alone, but not when the owner of the shop was there. Mr. Sowerberry liked Oliver. He thought the boy had a nice face. He especially liked the look of sadness about him.

After Oliver had been there a month, Mr. Sowerberry decided to have him take part in the funerals. He gave Oliver a hat and coat to wear, and Oliver walked with Mr. Sowerberry on many occasions. This made Noah Claypole very jealous. He tried to hurt Oliver more often than before. Noah made Oliver miserable whenever he could.

One day, they were both in the

kitchen being fed by Mrs. Sowerberry. When she left the room, Noah grabbed Oliver by the hair and pulled on his ear. He was very disappointed that Oliver didn't

cry. So Noah decided to make him cry another way.

"Hey brat," Noah said, "how's your mother?"

"She's dead," replied Oliver quickly. "Don't you say anything about her to me!"

Oliver's face turned red when he said this, and he started to blink rapidly. Noah thought he must be about to cry. He laughed and said, "You know, brat, it's not your fault your mother was such a bad one."

Oliver was enraged. He leaped up, seized Noah by the throat, and shook him until his teeth chattered in his head. Then, putting all his force into one blow, he knocked Noah to the ground. A moment before, he had been a quiet, mild boy. But the insult to his mother had made him fierce.

"Help!" cried Noah. "He's trying to kill me!"

Mrs. Sowerberry ran back into the kitchen. She was a nasty woman who

always preferred to think badly of other people. When she saw Oliver glaring down at Noah and heard Noah's cries, she screamed, "The boy is dangerous! It's a wonder we haven't all been murdered by him already!"

She tried to take hold of Oliver, but he struggled and fought against her. "Quick, Noah!" she cried. "Run and get Mr. Bumble from the workhouse!"

Noah got up and ran quickly to the gate of the workhouse. "Mr. Bumble, Mr. Bumble!" he yelled. "Oliver Twist has tried to kill me! Come at once!"

When they entered the shop, Mr. Sowerberry was there. He listened in astonishment to what his wife had to say about Oliver Twist.

"Perhaps he is mad!" Mr. Sowerberry said at last.

"It's not madness," said Mr. Bumble sternly. "It's meat!"

"What?" exclaimed Mrs. Sowerberry.

"You've over-fed him, madam!" said Mr. Bumble. "If you had kept him on gruel such as we fed him in the workhouse, this would not have happened. You've made him headstrong and willful. He has spirit! A poor boy like him does not need spirit. He should always be humble and meek."

Now, although Mrs. Sowerberry had given Oliver a few scraps of meat, she had never over-fed him. But she smiled and said, "So! This is what comes of my being generous!"

Oliver was not given a chance to defend himself. Mrs. Sowerberry hit him

whenever he tried to speak. Mr. Bumble told the coffin-maker to whip the boy soundly, then starve him for a few days. Then he marched off.

Mr. Sowerberry sighed. He would have preferred not to follow Mr. Bumble's orders, but his wife insisted. After Oliver was whipped, he was left in the shop for the night.

When he was alone, Oliver sat for a

long time with his head in his hands. Then he got up and looked out the window.

It was a cold, dark night. The stars seemed farther away than they had ever been before. There was no wind. The shadows that lay on the ground were terribly still and death-like. Oliver tied up what few things he had in a handkerchief and sat down to wait for morning.

As soon as the first rays of light entered the room, Oliver opened the door and ran away. He never looked back. There was no one to whom he wanted to say goodbye.

Chapter

3

To London

Oliver walked nearly five miles into the country. Every time he saw someone coming towards him on the road, or up from behind, he hid in the bushes. It was noon before he sat down to rest beside a large stone marker. Until then, he had thought only of getting away and of not being caught. Now, for the first time, he began to think of where he should go.

On the marker, in bold letters followed by a big arrow, it said that the city of London was seventy miles away. Oliver said to himself, "London is such a huge city that no one, not even Mr. Bumble, could ever find me there!"

The old men in the workhouse had told him that no lad of spirit need go hungry in London. They said that there were many ways of making a living in the big city. Oliver decided it was just the place for a homeless boy like himself to go. He jumped up and started on his way. He was not at all sure he could walk that far, but he was determined to try.

Day after day, Oliver walked on. He begged at nearby cottages for food and

slept in the open air. His feet were soon sore and bleeding. He became so tired and weak that his legs trembled beneath him.

Once, he waited at the bottom of a steep hill until a stagecoach came up, and then he begged for help from the passengers. They told him to run after the coach if he wanted a half-penny. Poor Oliver tried, but couldn't run because of his sore feet. When the passengers saw

this, they put their money away and called him a lazy fool.

Oliver was often driven away from the villages where he begged. One innkeeper threatened to set his dog on him if he didn't move on.

After walking for seven days, Oliver limped slowly into a little town just outside London. There he sat, covered with dust, upon a cold doorstep. His loneliness hurt him even more than his hunger.

Oliver was there for some time when he noticed an odd-looking boy watching him from across the street. The boy was about his own age, but behaved more like a grown man. He wore a top hat, which seemed about ready to fall off at any moment, and a man's coat that reached almost to his feet. He was not only dressed strangely, but he spoke strangely, too. He rambled over to Oliver and said,

"Hey covey, what's the row?"

Oliver guessed what he meant and said, "I am very tired. I have been walking for seven days."

"I suppose you'd like some food and a place to sleep tonight," said the boy in a friendly way.

Oliver said he would like that very much.

"Come then," said the boy, helping him up.

The boy said his name was Jack, but everyone called him "the artful Dodger." He bought some bread and ham at a shop, giving half of it to Oliver.

Then he said he knew a "nice old

gentleman" in London who would be happy to help Oliver find work.

Oliver was very puzzled by the boy. He wondered what he could be so good at "dodging" to deserve such an odd nickname. Also, the boy seemed to know, without being told, why Oliver had come to London. But Oliver was so thankful for the boy's help that he didn't ask any questions.

"The artful Dodger" led Oliver through many narrow, crooked streets to a dirty place where all the houses were old and falling apart. Suddenly, he took him by the arm and pulled him into one of the houses, slamming the door behind them. He brought Oliver up a dark, bro-

ken stairway and into a back room where a shriveled old man stood in front of a fire. The old man was toasting sausages on a long fork.

He had an ugly face, much of which

was hidden by his long, matted hair, and he was dressed in a loose robe. Several boys sat at a table near him, smoking long clay pipes. Like "the artful Dodger," they seemed to act more like men than

boys. On the floors of the dirty rooms were scattered many rough beds made of old sacks.

"Hey, Fagin," called "the artful Dodger" to the old man, "this is my new pal, Oliver Twist." Then he went up and whispered in the old man's ear.

"We are very glad to meet you, Oliver," said the old man with a wide grin on his face. "Come sit down and have something to eat."

When he sat down, a boy at the table started to go through Oliver's pockets— much to his surprise. But Fagin stopped the boy by poking him with the fork.

Countless silk handkerchiefs hung on a wooden rack at the end of the room. Fagin noticed Oliver staring at them and said, "We've a lot of handkerchiefs, haven't we, Oliver? We have just put them all out to wash."

The boys shouted and laughed at this. Oliver was not at all sure why, but he smiled and ate his supper eagerly.

Fagin gave Oliver a cup of something hot to drink. After he had finished it, Oliver felt very sleepy. Fagin then put Oliver to bed.

Oliver did not wake up until late the next morning. There was no one else in the room except Fagin. Oliver was very

drowsy. Although he was not asleep, he was not awake either. He thought he was still dreaming. His eyes were only half-open.

While he lay there, Oliver saw Fagin open a trap door in the floor and take out a heavy box. The old man's eyes seemed to shine brightly as he raised the lid. He took out a splendid gold watch, sparkling with jewels, and held it up to the light. He took out at least half a dozen watches, and many rings and bracelets, before he suddenly turned and saw that Oliver was looking at him. The old man closed the box with a crash and, picking up a knife from the table, grabbed Oliver angrily by the hair.

"Why are you watching me?" Fagin cried.

"I wasn't able to sleep any longer, sir," Oliver stammered in a sleepy voice.

Fagin put the knife down just as suddenly as he had picked it up and told Oliver he had been joking.

"I was only trying to frighten you a little, my dear," the old man chuckled. "You're a brave boy, Oliver. Did you see any of these pretty things?" he asked, laying his hand on the box.

"Yes sir," replied Oliver.

Fagin became very pale. "They're all mine Oliver. This is all I have to live on in my old age. You understand, don't you? Now, bring that pitcher of water over here and get washed."

Oliver went and got the water. When he returned, the box was gone.

Soon afterwards, "the artful Dodger" came in with one of the boys whom Oliver had seen smoking the night before. His name was Charley.

"Well," said Fagin cheerfully, "I hope you've been at work this morning, my dears."

"Hard at work," replied the Dodger.

"Good boys! Good boys!" exclaimed the old man. "What have you got to show me?"

The Dodger handed him two leather wallets, and Charley gave him two silk handkerchiefs.

"These are well-made," Fagin said, as he inspected them. "You'd like to learn how to make wallets and handkerchiefs, too, wouldn't you Oliver?"

"Oh yes, sir," Oliver said quickly.

Charley burst into laughter when he said this. Oliver looked at him in surprise. He didn't know what there was to laugh about.

Oliver sat and watched as Fagin, "the artful Dodger," and Charley played a strange game. The old man placed a wallet in one pocket of his trousers, a silk handkerchief in the other, and a watch on a long chain in a little pocket of his vest. Then he walked up and down the room, pretending that he was a rich, old gentleman in the city.

Sometimes Fagin would stop and stare into the fireplace, or the doorway, as if he were staring into a shop window. All this time, the two boys followed him closely, without ever letting him see where they were. At last, the Dodger moved in swiftly and stepped on the old man's toes, while Charley stumbled into him from behind. Before Oliver could say a word, the boys had taken Fagin's wallet, handkerchief, and watch.

Fagin looked so funny when he slapped his pockets and screamed that his wallet was gone. Oliver couldn't help but laugh and laugh.

Chapter

4

The Chase

After several days, Oliver became very tired of staying indoors with Fagin. He begged to be allowed to go out and work with "the artful Dodger" and Charley. He wanted to be useful, and longed to start making wallets and silk handkerchiefs, too.

Finally, one morning, Fagin said that Oliver could go out with the two boys. Oliver was very excited and happy. He wondered where they were going and what he would learn to make first. But "the artful Dodger" and Charley walked at such a lazy pace that Oliver soon decided they were going to fool the old man and not work at all. He was surprised, too, to see Charley stealing apples from the fruit sellers that they passed. Oliver was just about to say that he was going to turn back, when the Dodger made a sudden stop.

"What's the matter?" demanded Oliver.

"Hush!" replied the Dodger. "Do you see that bloke at the bookseller's?"

"That old gentleman over there?" asked Oliver. "Yes, I see him."

"He'll do," said the Dodger, and Charley nodded. The two of them crept up behind the old gentleman, and Oliver watched them in silent amazement.

The old gentleman was very well-dressed in a green coat with a black velvet collar and white trousers. He had picked up a book from the display in front of him and was reading it with great interest. He looked so content that he seemed to have forgotten where he was, and thought, instead, that he was home, sitting and reading in his favorite armchair.

Oliver was horrified to see the Dodger reach into the old gentleman's pocket, pull out a handkerchief, and hand it to Charley. Then they both ran away around the corner. Now Oliver understood Fagin's strange game! All the wallets and silk handkerchiefs that the boys brought in—all the gold watches and jewels that Fagin had taken out of the trap door in the floor . . . had been stolen!

Poor Oliver was so confused and ter-

rified that he didn't stop to think of what he should do. He turned from the bookseller's shop and started running away as fast as he could.

The very second that Oliver began to run, the old gentleman put his hand into his pocket and found that his handkerchief was missing. He wheeled around and caught sight of Oliver running away. He believed Oliver was the thief!

"Stop thief!" the gentleman shouted with all his might. He ran after Oliver, waving in his hand the book he had been reading. A crowd of people from the market place dropped what they were doing and joined in the chase. "Stop thief! Stop

thief!" they screamed. Away they ran, down alleys, around corners, from one street to another.

Finally, Oliver was overtaken by a man in a top hat who knocked him to the ground. He lay covered with mud and dust. His mouth was bleeding. He looked

wildly up at the faces who surrounded him.

The old gentleman who had been robbed was the only one who felt pity for Oliver. He looked down on the boy's gentle face in surprise and sorrow. The others clapped their hands and cheered the man

who had hit Oliver. Suddenly, a police officer arrived, grabbed Oliver by the collar,
and dragged him to his feet.

"It wasn't me, sir," pleaded Oliver
weakly. "It was the other two boys. They
are here somewhere."

"Ha!" the police officer laughed.

"Oh, please do not hurt him," said the old gentleman. "Why, now I am not sure that this boy took my handkerchief after all."

But the police officer would not listen to him. "It's too late now," he said. "You must both go before the judge."

Oliver was thrown into a cold jail cell until he had to appear in court. The old gentleman waited in the courthouse.

"That boy reminds me of someone," the man said to himself, tapping his chin with the cover of his book in a thoughtful manner. "I know I have seen a look like that before, but where?"

After what seemed to be a very long time, Oliver was dragged in front of a stern-faced judge who shook his finger at him and spoke harshly. Oliver was so sick and weak that he could hardly stand.

The judge's voice sounded muffled and far away to him; Oliver couldn't understand what was being said. He didn't know that the old gentleman who had been robbed was begging the judge to treat Oliver kindly.

The old gentleman, whose name was Mr. Brownlow, declared he was not sure that Oliver had stolen his handkerchief.

"The boy has been hurt," said Mr.

Brownlow, "and he looks very ill. I am afraid he will fall down."

"None of your tricks here, young man," the judge sneered at Oliver. "What's your name, boy?"

Suddenly, Oliver fell to the floor.

"What will you do with him now?"

cried Mr. Brownlow in great distress to the judge.

"I'll put him in prison. He'll have three months of hard labor," replied the judge.

The police officer was just about to pick Oliver up and carry him off to jail, when a little old man rushed into the courtroom.

"Stop! Stop! Don't take him away!

Please wait a moment!" he cried breathlessly.

"You are not supposed to be here," growled the judge. "Get out!"

"I will not be turned away! I will stay!" cried the little old man. "I own the book shop, and I saw it all happen. You must not refuse to hear me!"

"Oh, what have you got to say, old man?" asked the judge wearily.

"I saw three boys—two others besides the prisoner here," said the little old man, pointing to Oliver. "The handkerchief was taken by another boy. I could see that this boy was amazed by the robbery."

"Why didn't you come here before?" asked the judge.

"There was no one to look after my shop for me," explained the little old man. "Everybody I know had joined in the chase after this boy. I couldn't get anyone to help me until five minutes ago, and then I ran all the way here."

"Clear the court!" yelled the judge

angrily. "This has been a waste of my time! Put the boy out on the street and clear the court!"

Mr. Brownlow and the little old man who owned the book shop hurried out the door. "I-I am so sorry this had to happen!" stammered Mr. Brownlow. "If only I had not become so interested in reading this book outside your shop! Oh dear, there is the boy lying on the pavement!" Oliver's face was a deadly white, and he trembled from head to foot.

"He is terribly ill!" cried Mr. Brownlow.

The owner of the book shop hailed a cab, and the two men lifted Oliver inside.

"Please hurry, my good man," Mr. Brownlow shouted to the driver. "There is no time to lose!"

Chapter

5

Followed!

After "the artful Dodger" and Charley had stolen Mr. Brownlow's handkerchief, they "dodged" into a nearby doorway to hide until all the excitement was over. They saw Mr. Brownlow chase Oliver and knew that the boy would be arrested by the police.

"Ha! Ha! Ha!" laughed Charley, as they made their way home together. "To see him running away at that pace, with the crowd after him, and all the time I have the wipe in my pocket—oh, it's too much!"

"Be quiet! Do you want to get grabbed by the police? What'll Fagin say about this?" the Dodger asked in a voice full of fear.

Charley made no reply, but he stopped laughing.

Fagin was standing over the fire when he heard the sound of their footsteps echoing on the creaking stairs.

"Where's Oliver?" he demanded, as soon as they walked in. "What's become of the boy? Speak out or I'll thrash you!"

"Why, the traps have got him, that's all," said the Dodger. Then he twisted himself loose, snatched up the toasting fork, and darted around, trying to stab the old man with it. Fagin stepped back, picked up a pot of beer, and meant to throw it at the boy, but he hit someone else instead.

"Why, who threw that thing at me?" growled a deep voice from the darkness of

the doorway. A short, strong-looking man in a battered hat with a nasty scowl on his face had arrived in the middle of their quarrel. A dirty, white dog with a scratched face followed him into the room.

"What are you up to now, Fagin?" the man sneered. "Treating the boys badly, are you? It's a wonder they don't all murder you. I would if I was one of them and had to take orders from you!"

"Hush, Mr. Sikes," said the old man fearfully. "Don't speak so loudly!"

"Don't 'mister' me!" the man growled. "You know what my name is. Say it!"

"All right, then—Bill Sikes," said Fagin meekly. "Come sit down, Bill, and have a drink."

When both Bill Sikes and Fagin were seated with drinks in front of them, the Dodger told the story of Oliver's capture by the police.

"I'm afraid he may talk to the police about us," said Fagin, "and get us all into trouble. We've planned so many robberies together, Bill. If I was taken by the police, you'd surely be taken too."

"We must find out what's happened to him," said Bill Sikes in a very low voice. "We must send someone over to the courthouse to ask about him. If he is not in jail, then we must find out where he is, and grab him the first chance we get."

Meanwhile, a cab was rolling away from the courthouse in great haste, through many of the same streets that Oliver had walked with the Dodger when he first came into London. At last, the cab turned onto a quiet, shady street and stopped in front of a neat-looking brick house where Mr. Brownlow lived.

The old gentleman gathered Oliver into his arms and carried him up to a comfortable bed in a large, sunny room. Oliver was watched over and cared for with loving attention by Mr. Brownlow's housekeeper, a grey-haired woman named Mrs. Bedwin. But, for many days, he knew nothing of the kindness of his new friends. He lay, trembling with fever, without seeing or hearing anything that went on around him. Finally, he awoke from what seemed to have been a long and troubled sleep.

"Where am I?" said Oliver weakly. "This is not the place I went to sleep in."

"Hush dear," said Mrs. Bedwin softly. "You must rest quietly if you are to get well again." With those words, the old lady very gently placed Oliver's head upon the pillow, and smoothed his hair from his face.

In three days time, Oliver was well enough to sit up. Mrs. Bedwin carried him downstairs and placed him in an armchair, propped up with pillows.

"Are you very fond of pictures, dear?" Mrs. Bedwin asked. Oliver was staring most intently at the portrait of a lady which hung on the wall.

"I have seen so few that I really don't know," he said. "What a beautiful, mild face that lady has!"

The old lady looked at him and smiled. Just then, Mr. Brownlow walked into the room. Oliver told the old gentleman that he was very happy, and very grateful for all his goodness.

Mr. Brownlow was about to reply when he suddenly glanced up and

exclaimed, "Good heavens, Oliver! You look so very much like the woman in that picture that it takes my breath away!"

Mr. Brownlow was very eager to question Oliver about his past and find out how he came to be in the company of thieves. But he wanted to wait until the boy had fully recovered from his illness first. When he was well enough to get out of bed, Mr. Brownlow gave him a new suit of clothes. Everyone was so kind and gentle. It was like heaven to Oliver after his noisy, dirty life.

Not long after Oliver first saw the portrait of the lady, Mr. Brownlow asked to speak to him in his study. He asked Oliver about his past. Afterwards, he began teaching Oliver, in order to prepare him for school.

Oliver had been in the room a good while when Mrs. Bedwin entered with a small parcel of books. They were from the same bookseller who had helped Oliver in court.

"Oh dear!" cried Mr. Brownlow. "He has left, and I wanted to pay him the money that I owe him."

"Please let me bring it to him, sir," cried Oliver eagerly. "I will return as soon as I can."

Mr. Brownlow was about to say that

Oliver should not go out yet, but then he smiled, gave him the money, and told him to hurry after the bookseller.

Oliver didn't know he was being followed on his way to the marketplace by "the artful Dodger" and Bill Sikes. He was walking along, thinking of how happy he felt, when a pair of strong hands around his neck stopped him.

"Let go of me," Oliver cried as he

struggled. "Help! Help!" But there was no one to hear his screams. "The artful Dodger" grinned at him. Bill Sikes's mean little dog snapped at his ankles and looked as if he would like to tear into his throat.

"If you so much as say a word, I'll set the dog on you," growled Bill Sikes. "Now, take hold of my hand." Oliver was pulled through many dark, narrow streets to the crooked old house where Fagin lived.

"Glad to see you looking so well, my dear," Fagin laughed. The Dodger went through Oliver's pockets and took the money that was meant for the bookseller.

"I'll take that money," said Fagin.

"Oh, please don't," pleaded Oliver. "It is from the kind, old gentleman who helped me when I was dying from fever. Please send it back to him. He and Mrs. Bedwin will think that I stole it!"

"Ha! Ha! That's right, Oliver! They will think you stole it!" the old man cackled.

"That's right, Oliver!" repeated Bill Sikes. "And they won't send the police after you either—for fear you should be thrown in jail!"

While these words were being spoken, Oliver looked from one to the other in disbelief. He was afraid of them both, but he forgot his fear when he thought that kind Mr. Brownlow and Mrs. Bedwin would think him a liar and a thief. He jumped suddenly to his feet and ran wildly from the room, screaming for help. But he was stopped by the Dodger. Then Fagin

grabbed him and held him while Bill Sikes beat him.

Mr. Brownlow and Mrs. Bedwin waited until long after dark for Oliver to return. They were fearful, but Sikes was right. They didn't send for the police.

Chapter

6

A House
in the Country

Oliver was forced to stay inside with Fagin for many days. But very early one morning, the old man suddenly pulled Oliver out of bed and brought him to a tavern where they met Bill Sikes and another man, Toby Crackit.

Oliver was terrified when Bill Sikes growled at him. "If you speak a word when you're with me, I'll put a bullet in your head!"

Then Sikes and Toby, with Oliver between them, walked out of the city. They traveled on country roads and only stopped to rest in places where they were well hidden. It became dark, and Oliver expected to stop for the night, but still they walked on.

Finally, they stopped at a house surrounded by a high, brick wall. Toby climbed the wall and held out his arms for Oliver. In another minute, all three of

them were lying on the grass on the other side. And then, for the first time, Oliver knew that he was to take part in a robbery! He looked up at Sikes and was about to scream, but the man put a pistol to his head and pointed to a little window that was at the back of the house.

"I'll put you in there," he said. "Then you walk across the hall, unlock the door, and let us in."

Bill Sikes reminded Oliver that he was within his sight all the way to the door. If he didn't do as he was told, Sikes would shoot him with the pistol.

Oliver decided that, even if he was shot in the attempt, he would try to dart up the stairs and warn the family. He started forward.

All at once, there was a noise from above and Bill Sikes cried, "Come back! Back! Back!"

A light appeared, and Oliver saw two terrified, half-dressed men at the top of the stairs. Then there was a flash—a loud noise—smoke. Oliver staggered back. Sikes grabbed him by the collar and dragged him out of the little window.

"They've hit the boy," he cried. "Oh, how he bleeds!" Sikes quickly wrapped Oliver's wounded arm in a scarf.

Then came the loud ringing of a bell, the sound of pistol shots, and the shouting of men. Sikes carried Oliver some distance. But then, when he heard footsteps close behind him, he dropped the boy and ran on by himself. Toby was ahead of him.

Oliver lay there until morning, when he moaned in pain and awoke. After a long time, he was able to stand. He was dizzy and staggered like a drunken man. He saw the house and remembered that

they had tried to rob it. This made him so afraid that he almost forgot the pain in his arm. But, he had to seek help at the house; there was no other in sight. He stumbled across the lawn and over to the door. He knocked faintly, and then he fell down in a daze.

The two servants whom Oliver had seen the night before on the stairs opened the door.

"Here he is!" one of them called up the stairs.

"Here's one of the thieves, ma'am! I wounded him!"

"Hush!" replied a young lady on the

stairs behind them, "or you will frighten my aunt with your loud shouting. Is the poor creature hurt badly?"

The young lady was soon joined by a much older woman who was very distressed to see a boy, lying hurt, in her doorway. She ordered that he be put to bed upstairs, and she asked one of the servants to run for the doctor.

In a short while, a carriage drove up to the garden gate. A stout gentleman jumped out of it and rushed up to the door. It was Dr. Losberne. He was a good friend of both Mrs. Maylie, the old woman who owned the house, and her adopted niece, Rose. For the second time in Oliver's life, he had fallen into the hands of kind, good-hearted people. He lay, dazed and in terrible pain, while Dr. Losberne bandaged his arm.

After they left Oliver's room, Mrs. Maylie cried, "That poor boy could never have been a thief!"

Dr. Losberne shook his head sadly

and said, "I am afraid there are many
thieves his age in the city."

"But even if he has been wicked,
remember that he may never have known

a mother's love or the comfort of a home,"
cried Rose. "He may have been driven to
steal by hunger. Oh, my dear aunt! If it
had not been for your goodness, I may

have been left—just like this poor child—alone and helpless in the world. Please help him for my sake!"

Mrs. Maylie turned to the doctor. "What can I do? The servants have already sent for the police."

"Let us make an agreement," said Dr. Losberne. "The boy will awaken in an hour or so. Then, I will question him in your presence. If, from what he says, we decide that he is really a bad one—which is very possible—we will tell the police

and let them take him to prison. But if he is worthy of our help and regard, I think I can convince your servants that he might not have been one of the thieves after all."

Rose smiled and Mrs. Maylie clapped her hands in satisfaction.

It was evening before Oliver could speak to them. He was very weak and tired, but he told them all about his life up to that time. He told them, too, of how much he had wanted to run up the stairs and warn them of the robbery before he had been shot.

When Oliver had finished, Dr. Losberne wiped some tears from his eyes and rushed downstairs to speak to the servants. They were both very proud that they had stopped one of the thieves. But Dr. Losberne told them that he was not at all sure that the boy upstairs was a thief. The doctor thundered at the servants with his loud voice, and confused them so much that, finally, when the police came, they said that they had been mistaken about the boy.

Oliver was very, very ill. Dr. Losberne had to see him every day. In addition to the wound he had received in his arm, he had been out in the wet and cold all night. He had a fever for many weeks. But at last, he began to get better and was able to say how very grateful he was for the goodness of the two ladies who took care of him. He said that he wanted to grow well and strong in order to prove that he was indeed worthy of their kindness.

Chapter

7

A Strange Meeting

Oliver was very happy and content with Mrs. Maylie and Rose. But even so, he had not forgotten Mr. Brownlow and Mrs. Bedwin in London. He longed to see them and tell them how happy he was. He worried that they might still think of him as an ungrateful liar and thief. Dr. Losberne promised to take Oliver to visit them as soon as he was well enough to make such a long journey.

At last the day arrived. Oliver and Dr. Losberne set out together in a small carriage. Oliver knew the name of the quiet, shady street on which Mr. Brownlow lived, and the driver was instructed to go directly there.

When the carriage finally turned onto the street, Oliver became so excited that he could not sit still. The doctor smiled and patted him gently.

Oliver pointed to the right house, and prepared to jump out of the carriage and run up the stairs. But...the Brownlow house was empty! A sign in the window said that the house was for rent.

The doctor inquired at the house next door for news of the old gentleman and discovered that both he and Mrs. Bedwin had left on a ship for the West Indies. Oliver was disappointed. The doctor sighed, telling the driver to return home immediately.

In the past, Oliver's days had always been spent among noisy, dirty crowds of people. There, in the country, he felt almost as if he was beginning a new life.

Every morning, he walked over to the cottage of a pleasant, old gentleman who taught him to read and write. When he returned, he would either listen as Rose

sang or read aloud, or help Mrs. Maylie in the garden. In the evening, he would prepare his lessons for the next day. He usually worked in a little room in the back of the house. His desk there was beside a window which was framed with vines of sweet-smelling honeysuckle.

One beautiful evening, when the summer light was just beginning to fade, Oliver sat reading at the window. He had been working very hard and, little by little,

he fell asleep. But although he dozed, he was still aware of what was going on around him.

Suddenly, the air seemed to become musty. He could no longer smell the honeysuckle outside his window. Oliver thought, with terror, that he was in Fagin's house again. He thought he could hear Fagin whispering to someone about him.

Oliver awoke with a start and looked

up. To his horror, he realized that he had not only been dreaming, but Fagin was at his window! Next to him stood a mean-looking man with a long, pointed nose whom Oliver had never seen before. The two of them turned and were gone in an instant. Oliver leaped into the garden and cried loudly for help.

Fagin had been angry when he learned that Bill Sikes had left Oliver, wounded, outside the Maylie house. He wanted the robber to return for the boy.

A week after Oliver saw him at the window, Fagin went to the rooms above the tavern where Bill Sikes usually stayed. He found a young woman, wrapped in a shawl, staring sadly into the fire.

"Oh, it's you, Nancy," Fagin said in surprise. "I haven't seen you in a very long time."

"Not long enough for me, Fagin," said the woman bitterly, without even turning her head. Nancy had once been a thief for

Fagin, when she was just a little girl.

Fagin shrugged. "Where do you think Bill is?" he asked. "I saw the child and he is well again. Bill must bring him back to me. Did you hear what I said, Nancy? I must speak to Bill about Oliver Twist!"

Nancy turned and said, "The child is better where he is than among us. Leave him! If he hasn't spoken to the police by now, he never will!" Then she sank back into her chair and stared at the fire again.

Fagin was enraged because Nancy would not help him find Bill Sikes.

"What?" he cried, shaking his fist at her. "Leave him? When the boy is worth so much money to me!" Suddenly, Fagin stopped and put his hand over his mouth. He looked around quickly. Nancy had not moved. Fagin didn't know whether she had heard him or not.

"Nancy, my dear," he said in a pleasant voice, "you were not listening to me just then, were you?"

Nancy mumbled that she never bothered to listen to him anymore. Fagin then turned to go, saying that he could not wait for Bill Sikes to return.

Fagin went home to find a man wrapped in a dark cloak, standing outside his door. He was the same man that Oliver had seen outside his window whispering with Fagin.

As the two men went upstairs, they were followed by Nancy. She moved very quietly and stayed in the shadows close

to the wall where they could not see her. She had only pretended not to hear what Fagin had said about Oliver. She knew that he was planning to use the boy for some evil purpose and decided to try and find out what it was. Nancy did not want Fagin to ruin Oliver's life in the same way that he had ruined hers.

Fagin took the man into his room. He knew that no one, except one of the thieves who worked for him, could find them there. They sat down at the table, to talk.

"Well, Monks," Nancy heard Fagin say to the stranger, "we saw the boy ourselves."

"Why couldn't you have kept him here and turned him into a thief like the other boys?" asked the man called Monks. "Why did you ever send him out on that robbery in the first place?"

"It wasn't that easy," said Fagin. "He isn't like other boys. But don't worry. We will get him back. Did you find the workhouse where he was born?"

"Yes. I gave some money to a police officer there named Bumble and found out all I needed to know. They have no idea who the parents of Oliver Twist were. If all goes well, I will be able to keep his fortune for myself," replied Monks.

"Everything will go well," cried Fagin eagerly. "No one will ever find out who the boy really is, and I will make him a thief, and he will steal for me!"

"If you do, I will pay you a great deal of money. First, however, you must get him back again. There is no need to send Bill Sikes all the way into the country. They are all here in London for a few weeks. The old woman has some business to attend to. It amazes me that the boy has fallen into the same household with Rose Maylie. If only they knew..."

Suddenly, Monks cried out and pointed to the wall. "Fagin, look! I saw a woman's shadow!"

"Calm yourself," said Fagin. "You are always becoming excited over nothing. We are alone."

Chapter

8

Nancy

After Monks saw her shadow on the wall, Nancy disappeared down the stairs and ran all the way back to the tavern. She was very excited, but she tried not to show it.

When she got home, she was so pale, and her eyes were so bright that Bill Sikes asked her if she had a fever. She had to stay with him, but she planned to go and speak to Rose Maylie. She had to tell Rose what Fagin and Monks had said about Oliver.

Nancy wanted to help Oliver very much, but she did not wish to have Fagin or Bill Sikes arrested. She did not want to betray them, even if they were mean and cruel, because they were the only friends she had ever known.

On the following night, Nancy gave Bill Sikes a hot drink. She put something in it to make him feel tired. When, at last, he fell asleep, she started on her way to see Rose Maylie.

Nancy had overheard Monks tell Fagin the name of the hotel where the family was staying. She rushed there, knocking into people on her way and darting between the heads of horses in the streets. She seemed to have no concern for her own safety. The people who passed by her thought she must be mad.

Rose was very surprised when Nancy was shown into her room. But she was even more surprised by what Nancy had to tell her. Nancy spoke quickly. She had to hurry back to the tavern before she was missed. If Fagin or Bill Sikes knew where she had been, they would surely make her suffer for it.

"But why do you wish to return to such people?" Rose cried. "We will help you to a place of safety far away from them if you will only let us!"

"Dear lady!" cried Nancy. "If I had only heard such words when I was a girl, I might have been saved from this kind of life. Now it is too late!"

"But where can I speak to you

again?" asked Rose. "There must be a place where we can meet."

"Every Sunday night, between eleven and midnight, I will walk on London Bridge... if I am alive," said Nancy. Then she rushed out of the room.

Mrs. Maylie and Oliver had walked to a park. Rose decided to sit down and write to Dr. Losberne for advice. Although she wanted very much to discover the truth about Oliver's parents and learn of the fortune that Monks had spoken of,

she did not want to do anything that would place Nancy in danger. As she was writing, Oliver entered the room and called to her in such an excited, breathless way, that she became alarmed.

"What is the matter?" she cried anxiously.

"I saw Mr. Brownlow in the park and ran up to speak to him. He is here now!" Oliver answered.

Rose hurried into the parlor to meet the kind old gentleman. Oliver was impa-

tient to see Mrs. Bedwin again. So, Mr. Brownlow offered to take them over to his new lodgings. While Oliver visited with the housekeeper, Rose told Mr. Brownlow all that she had heard from Nancy.

"We must be very cautious," Mr. Brownlow said. "We will never get to the bottom of this mystery unless we can learn more about this man, Monks. On Sunday night, we will ask Nancy to point out Monks to us. If she cannot do so, we will ask her to describe what he looks like and name a place where he can be found."

It was decided that no one, besides Mrs. Maylie and Dr. Losberne, should know of the matter. Not even Oliver would learn of it—unless they were able to discover the truth about his past.

There was now someone new in Fagin's gang. It was Noah Claypole, the boy who had worked with Oliver in Mr. Sowerberry's shop and had tried to make him cry on the night before he ran away.

Noah had stolen all the money in the coffin-maker's shop before going to London. He was very glad to work for Fagin, and he hoped to make his fortune as a thief.

On Sunday night, Fagin arrived at the tavern to speak to Bill Sikes. While they sat whispering at the table, the clock struck the hour—eleven o'clock. Nancy got up nervously and put on her bonnet.

"Why, where do you think you're going at this time of night?" demanded Sikes.

"I'm not well," said Nancy. "I want a breath of fresh air."

"Open the window then," growled Sikes.

"I must go into the street," said Nancy. "I won't be gone long."

Sikes rose from the table and stomped across the room. He locked the door and took away the key. Then he pulled the bonnet from Nancy's head and threw it on the floor.

"You'll stay here!" he shouted.

"What do you mean by this, Bill?" Nancy cried. "You must let me go!"

Sikes seized her roughly by the arm and forced her to sit in a chair. She struggled with him until the clock struck twelve. Then she knew that she could no longer meet Rose on London Bridge.

Rose and Mr. Brownlow waited for Nancy until it was very late. They were

very worried about her when she did not come.

Fagin eyed Nancy strangely as he prepared to leave that night. He thought that she must have been planning to meet someone. Why else would she have struggled so violently against Bill Sikes? The next morning, he met secretly with Noah Claypole and told him that he had a very special job for him to do. He wanted

Noah to follow Nancy and spy on her.

"Tell me where she goes, who she sees, and what she says," Fagin said.

A week later, on Sunday night, Sikes was not at the tavern with Nancy. Fagin had sent him on a robbery so that he could not prevent Nancy from keeping her appointment. After eleven, Noah followed her to the bridge. It was a dark, foggy night. He hid in shadows. Nancy did not notice him.

Nancy met Rose and Mr. Brownlow and led them down some stone steps at the end of the bridge, where she thought that they could not be seen.

"I couldn't come last Sunday night. I was kept at the tavern—by force!" she said.

Rose told Nancy how very worried they had been about her. Then Mr. Brownlow asked if she could point Monks out to them. Nancy said she could not do that, but she could describe what he looked like. When she had finished, Mr.

Brownlow declared that he thought he knew the man... but by a different name!

Rose and Mr. Brownlow begged to be allowed to help Nancy in some way, but she told them that there was nothing that could be done for her. Then she hurried away into the darkness.

After they had parted company, Noah Claypole ran back to Fagin as fast as his legs would carry him. He told the old man all that he had heard.

While Noah slept, Fagin waited for Bill Sikes to come in.

"At last! At last!" he muttered when he heard Sikes's footsteps on the stairs.

Sikes threw a bundle on the table in front of Fagin. The old man grabbed it and locked it in a cupboard. Then he poured the robber a drink.

"Why are you looking at me so strangely?" growled Sikes. "What have you got on your mind?"

Fagin raised his hand, and shook his trembling finger in the air. But he was so upset that he could not speak. He stared at Sikes with wide eyes.

Bill Sikes grabbed him by the collar and shook him. "Speak!" he shouted. "Speak! Tell me what it is you've got to say!"

Fagin pointed to Noah Claypole in the bed and said, "What would you do, Bill, if that lad there were to tell on all of us? What if he described us to the right people and told where we could be found? What if he told them about a job that we had done?"

Sikes shook his fist at the boy. "If he was still alive when I found him, I would crush his skull with the iron heel of my boot!"

"And what if someone else were to do such a thing," asked Fagin eagerly.

"I would do the same thing, no matter who it was," Bill Sikes shouted.

Fagin then got Noah out of bed and had him tell Sikes everything that he had seen Nancy do. When he had heard all, Bill Sikes jumped up with a yell and flung on his coat. Fagin tried to say something to him, but he pushed the old man out of his way and darted wildly down the stairs. He did not pause once, not until

he had reached the room where Nancy lay asleep. She awoke with a start.

"Get up!" he growled fiercely. "You were watched tonight. Every word you said was overheard!"

"Bill! Bill!" cried Nancy. "I did nothing that could hurt you! Please hear me!"

Bill Sikes grabbed his club and came at Nancy with all his force. She tried to

defend herself but soon stumbled to the ground. She stared at him with wild eyes, and put out her hand to him. Then she fell over.

Of all the bad deeds that had been committed in London that dark night, Nancy's death was the worst. It was the most cruel. Bill Sikes was filled with terror by what he had done. He kept imagining Nancy's eyes following him around the room. He kept seeing her face before him—the way it had been just before she staggered and fell. Finally, he ran from the room.

He walked out of the city and into the country. He rambled through fields and meadows and lay down to rest under hedges. His shaggy, dirty, white dog followed at his heels. He wandered over miles and miles of ground before deciding to return to London and hide at Fagin's house.

He overheard in a village tavern that the police were looking for a strong man with a shaggy, white dog. In order that he would not be recognized, he decided to drown the dog. He wrapped a heavy stone in a handkerchief and walked to the edge of a nearby pond. He wanted to tie the stone to the dog and throw him in the water. He called to the animal. The dog looked up into his face and, as if it knew what he was planning to do, turned and bounded away across the fields.

"Come here!" cried Sikes angrily. But the dog did not return.

Chapter

9

The Murderer

As soon as Rose and Mr. Brownlow learned of Nancy's awful death, they went to the police. They told all they knew about Bill Sikes, Fagin, and his gang of thieves. Fagin, "the artful Dodger," Noah Claypole, and most of the other boys were arrested immediately, but the police could not find Bill Sikes anywhere.

The night that the murderer returned to London, Toby Crackit was hiding in a house near the tavern where Nancy had been killed. Toby had gone with Sikes to rob the Maylie house many weeks before.

There was a pattering noise on the ledge outside the window. Looking up,

Toby saw Sikes's dog jump into the room.

"Why," he thought fearfully to himself, "the dog must have gone first to Fagin's house, and then to the tavern. Finding them filled with strangers, it made its way here. Sikes will do the same. He and his dog will bring the police to my door!"

Suddenly, Bill Sikes burst into the room. Toby almost screamed in surprise and horror when he saw the murderer's face. Then he ran over to the window.

Sikes stared at him. "Have you nothing to say to me?" he asked gruffly. "How did the dog get here?"

"Hush!" cried Toby, pointing outside in alarm.

Sikes saw that there were lights moving below. A crowd was gathering. "They

must have seen the dog and followed it here," he moaned.

The building they were hiding in was surrounded by a deep ditch. When the tide came in, it became filled with water, like a moat. One had to cross a small bridge in order to get from the street to the house.

"Give me a rope," said Sikes. "I will lower myself into the water and swim away from here." Then, taking a rope from Toby, he climbed onto the roof.

A loud shout went up below. People pointed to him eagerly. They knew he was the murderer! Sikes tied the rope to a chimney and peered over the edge of the roof. But the water was out. The ditch was a rocky bed of mud!

More and more people gathered below. Sikes could hear shouting inside the house and knew that the police had broken into Toby's room. He decided to make one last effort to escape by lowering himself into the mud. He made a noose at

the end of a rope to put around his waist. Just when the noose was over his head, before he could slip it under his arms, he turned and looked behind him. He threw up his hands and screamed in terror. He saw the face of Nancy before him again, covered with blood. Her eyes were wide and staring.

"The eyes again! The eyes!" he shouted and fell backward. The noose was around his neck. He fell more than thirty feet before the rope tightened. There was a sudden jerk. Nancy's murderer swung, lifeless, in the air.

Sikes's dog had jumped out onto the roof after him. It howled when he fell and ran back and forth, as if it did not know which way to turn. Finally, it stopped at the edge of the roof and stared at the lifeless body hanging below. Then, it jumped. It tried to leap onto the dead man's shoulders, but missed. In another minute, it lay dead in the muddy ditch.

Chapter

10

The Truth

Dr. Losberne had set out for London as soon as he had received Rose Maylie's letter. With his help, Mr. Brownlow was able to find Monks, the man who had plotted with Fagin against Oliver. Mr. Brownlow threatened to tell the police all that he knew, unless Monks came quietly to his lodgings.

When they were inside, Mr. Brownlow said, "You call yourself Monks now, but I have known you by another name—Leeford. Your father was my friend. Now I know that he had two sons—you, and your half-brother, Oliver Twist! You have done everything you could to prevent

Oliver from inheriting the money that his father left him!"

Monks looked as if he wanted to run out the door, but Dr. Losberne was guarding it.

"I knew your mother well," continued Mr. Brownlow. "She was a mean, nasty woman who made your father miserable. After you were grown, he met Oliver's mother—a lovely, sweet woman named Agnes, with a young sister to care for. A few months before Oliver was born, your father was called away on important business to Rome. He became very ill there and died. You were with him at the time. You hid his will and claimed his fortune for yourself.

"Poor Agnes was on her way to London to seek advice from me when she was overtaken by robbers. They left her in the street penniless and alone. She walked on for as long as she could before she dropped to the ground in exhaustion. The police found her and brought her to the nearest workhouse, where she gave birth to a boy—Oliver.

"When you returned to England, you pretended to help me look for Agnes and her sister. You made me believe that Agnes, her child, and her sister, had all died. In fact, you paid someone to take Agnes's sister to a workhouse in a distant city. Later, she was adopted by a kind

woman named Mrs. Maylie. Yes! We know that Rose Maylie is Oliver's aunt!

"Chance brought Oliver to me in London. While he was at my house, I noticed his resemblance to Agnes in the portrait I have of her. You gave me that portrait. It had belonged to your father. You brought it back with you from Rome and left it with me. I began to suspect a connection between Oliver and yourself. I remembered that you had lived in the West Indies, and I went there in search of you. When I couldn't find you, I returned to London.

"You wanted Fagin to make Oliver

steal. You were willing to pay him to do so. That is because, according to your father's will, Oliver cannot inherit any money if he has committed a crime!"

Mr. Brownlow forced Monks to sign a paper stating that Oliver Twist was the son of his father, Edwin Leeford, and therefore, entitled to half his fortune. Then Monks was taken away by the police.

In the meantime, Fagin had been led away to a cold, stone jail cell where he was to remain until the day he would be hanged for his crimes. At his trial, crowds of people had pressed into the courtroom in order to see him. All regarded him with horror. When the judge announced that Fagin had been found guilty by the jury, and was sentenced to die on the gallows, a tremendous cheer shook the court-house.

As he sat alone in his cell, Fagin shuddered to recall all the men he had known who had died on the gallows.

Their faces rose up before him in the darkness. There were so many that he could hardly count them all. He had seen some of them die and had joked about it later. How quickly they had changed from powerful men to dangling heaps of clothes! Now Fagin was to die in the very same way!

Chapter

The truth about Oliver had remained hidden for a long time, and he had been forced to live among some very cruel and evil people. But when, at last, the truth was told, he was happily settled with a family who loved him dearly.

Not long after Mr. Brownlow's startling discovery about Oliver, another secret was revealed which no one had expected. Mrs. Maylie's son, who had been away for several months, returned home and announced that he and Rose planned to marry. After their wedding took place, Mrs. Maylie went with them to a quiet village in the country. Oliver was

not to be far away, however. Mr. Brownlow had adopted him as his own son and, together with Mrs. Bedwin, they went to live in the same village in a house that was only a short walk from the Maylies' cottage. There, they were to be very happy.

The good Dr. Losberne soon found

that he missed his friends very much. He, too, decided to take a house in the same village in order to be near them.

After the excitement they had known in the city, they all welcomed a peaceful life in the country. Mr. Brownlow took great delight in teaching Oliver every day. And Oliver, in turn, took great delight in learning from him. In the evening, when they had finished their studies, they would walk together to the Maylies' cottage where they would be met by Rose, smiling in the doorway.

Rose and Oliver had never expected to find out who their parents were. The happiness they now felt would last them both for the rest of their lives.

THE END

ABOUT THE AUTHOR

CHARLES DICKENS, born in England in 1812, was considered by many to be the greatest novelist of his country. He grew up the poor son of a Navy clerk. Unable to receive proper schooling, Dickens went to work in a factory at the age of twelve.

Dickens made up for his lack of schooling by working hard. He became an office boy in a law firm, and afterwards a reporter of English Parliament debates. Many of his papers were published, and by age twenty-four, Dickens was a well-known and successful author.

Many of Dickens's works focused on the hardships of living in the nineteenth century. His popular novels include *A Christmas Carol*, *David Copperfield*, and *A Tale of Two Cities*. Much of his later work was published in the two weekly periodicals that he founded. Dickens continued these publications until his death in 1870.

The Young Collector's
Illustrated Classics

Adventures of Robin Hood

Black Beauty

Call of the Wild

Dracula

Frankenstein

Heidi

Little Women

Moby Dick

Oliver Twist

Peter Pan

The Prince and the Pauper

The Secret Garden

Swiss Family Robinson

Treasure Island

20,000 Leagues Under the Sea

White Fang